Humphrey

and His Very Special Friends

Sandra L. O'Grady

Illustrated by

Jacqueline O'Grady

ASPIRE
PUBLISHING HUB LLC.

ISBN
978-1-964393-21-6 (Paperback)
978-1-964393-22-3 (eBook)
978-1-964393-20-9 (Hardcover)

DEDICATION

To God, the author and finisher of life, my two beautiful daughters Nicole and Jacqueline and to Andrew for all his help.

Humphrey and His Very Special Friends

What a wonderful day to be alive! The rain is pouring and the clouds are gray, but the possibilities are endless.

"Humphrey, would you kindly move over? You know, this bush isn't just yours. There are almost 200 of us snails living here."

"I know, Penelope. How would you like to slug over to our friends' house at Berry Bush Avenue?"

"It's raining birds and squirrels, Humphrey, not a good day for traveling."

"Penelope, we have our shells and our bush is just in front of their place."

"Hey, keep quiet you two. I'm trying to get some sleep."

"Sorry, Mr. Jefferies," the two snails said.

"Mr. Jefferies, would you like to come with me to our friends' house at Berry Bush Avenue?"

"No, Humphrey, I'm too old and the weather makes me feel grumpy."

"Mr. Jefferies, you're not too old, you're just experienced. Gray skies don't last forever!"

The rain continued to pour and lightning lit up the sky, but that didn't discourage Humphrey any.

"Mom, would you like to come with me to visit our friends at Berry Bush Avenue?"

"Not now, Humphrey, I have too many chores to do. I'm too busy."

"Mom, didn't you say that sometimes you just need to make time for friends?"

"You're right Humphrey, I did say that. Let's get our raincoats on and go!"

Meanwhile over at Berry Bush Avenue, Grasshopper was helping his neighbor, Spider, weave a web.

"Grasshopper, I honestly wouldn't be able to survive without all your help"

"Oh Spider, my two legs may be crippled but I still have the use of my other four legs, and you, Spider, give great directions for weaving."

"There have been many times that I have let my arthritis get me down, but you, Grasshopper, have encouraged me to not give up. Thank you!"

"My pleasure, Spider!"

Just as a crash of thunder roared through Berry Bush Avenue, Humphrey, along with his mother, Patty, Penelope, and Mr. Jefferies, arrived at Berry Bush Avenue.

"Well welcome Humphrey and friends, what a wonderful surprise!" Buzzed Bee. "Ant could you please bring our guests some towels to dry off with?"

"Certainly," smiled Ant.

"Achoo!" Sneezed Bee.

"Bless you. Bee," said Humphrey.

"Thank you Humphrey. Ever since I tried to pollinate our flowers my allergies started acting up. Achoo!" Sneezed Bee again.

"Oh, Bee, it just doesn't seem fair. You being a bee and all, yet you're allergic to pollen." Sighed Patty.

"I sometimes start to feel sorry for myself, but then I realize how fortunate I really am. I do have my allergy medicine, and that does help a lot. Oh dear, I must check on Ant. After that terrible fall from Grasshopper's picnic table last summer, he just hasn't been the same. Ant took a pretty hard blow to the head, and well... he doesn't always understand directions. Excuse me please."

"Well if I was a bee and allergic to pollen, an ant who can't understand directions, a grasshopper who is crippled, and of all the things, a spider that has arthritis, I would just plain give up. That is what they should all do I tell you," grumbled Mr. Jefferies.

"Mr. Jefferies, how could you say that?" Asked Humphrey.

Spider and Grasshopper had just finished weaving a beautiful silk web. Both Spider and Grasshopper were in pain. Spider's arthritis flared up and Grasshopper's good legs were exhausted. The web was perfect!

Just then, a storm cloud erupted. Hail as big as acorns came crashing down.

Spider and Grasshopper were both complimenting each other's work, when hail fiercely tore through their web. The three days it had taken them to make the web, now had taken only minutes to be destroyed. There were only a few dangling threads that remained.

The whole crew rushed to Grasshopper and Spider to see if they had been injured. Humphrey, Patty, Penelope, Mr. Jefferies, Bee and Ant all stared in disbelief. Spider's web had been destroyed. Each one of them knew how bad Spider's arthritis was and how painful it was for Grasshopper to use his good legs for an extended amount of time. Bee and Ant had tears streaming down their faces.

"Oh Spider, how sad this is!" Cried Humphrey.

"Poor, poor dears," sobbed Patty.

"Just give up and move to one of those retirement homes!" Scoffed Mr. Jefferies.

"Life is just not fair," bawled Penelope.

"Oh please, please, friends, it's alright. I'm so very thankful that no one was injured. Besides, the doctor said that I need to be as active as possible, so that my arthritis won't get the best of me. I wouldn't have traded spending all this time with such a giving insect as Grasshopper," smiled Spider.

Just as Spider finished speaking, a brilliant rainbow flooded the sky. The storm had passed, and the rest of the afternoon was filled with possibilities. Each insect looked passed their disabilities and concentrated on their abilities; their ability to help and encourage one another, and the most important, to be thankful in all things.